I was a Teenage Vegetarian Zombie Detective

H. M. Gooden

Published by H. M. Gooden, 2019.

This is a work of fiction. Similarities to real people, places, or events are entirely coincidental.

I WAS A TEENAGE VEGETARIAN ZOMBIE DETECTIVE

First edition. October 11, 2019.

ISBN: 978-1989156179

Written by H. M. Gooden.

Also by H. M. Gooden

The Dragons of the North
Mai's First Date

The Raven and the Witch Hunter
The Raven and the Witch Hunter: The Spirit of Big Bear
The Raven and the Witch Hunter: The Wedding
The Raven and The Witch Hunter: Honeymoon and Full
Moon Blues
Wendigo

The Rise of the Light
Fiona's Gift
Dream of Darkness
The Stone Dragon
The Phoenix and the Witch
Dragons are Forever
The Raven and the Witch Hunter
Zahara's Quest

Standalone
The Raven and the Witch Hunter Omnibus: Volumes 2-4
To Capture the Heart of Spring
Darkness on the Nile
I was a Teenage Vegetarian Zombie Detective

Watch for more at https://www.hmgoodenauthor.com/.

Table of Contents

This one goes out to my #1 & #2.

They may not be as old as the characters in this book, but my Alex and Sam are just as entertaining, and I hope we'll have a relationship as good as the characters in my book.

(Without the supernatural drama, of course!)

And yes, they love zombies.

But only the cartoon ones, just like their mom.

Chapter 1

"This is not what I meant when I said I needed a Halloween costume."

Crossing my arms, I turned to glare at my best friend. She looked the same as always; big blue hipster glasses, dirty blonde hair in a messy ponytail, and wearing another one of her endless supply of T-shirts with math jokes.

When I looked back at the mirror, I couldn't help but shake my head at what I saw in front of me. The massive hollows under my eyes were new, as was the pale grey of my skin. I'd never won awards for my complexion, but this was an incredible low, even for me.

I had no idea what had happened the night before, but when I woke up this morning, I'd felt something was off. Not only did I smell way funkier than normal, but somehow my fingernails had become dirty overnight. When I picked the first leaf out of my hair I had instantly known something was terribly, terribly wrong.

You see, that was also the moment I'd realized I had no pulse.

So, I did what I do when anything goes wrong. I called Sam.

She'd been my best friend since kindergarten and lived in the house right beside me. It had been sheer luck she'd moved to town and next door to me when she had. We were both only

1

children, and as neither of our parents had any intention of adding a sibling for us to play with, when Sam had moved next door to me at age five, our mutual loneliness had bonded us together in the way that only the most lonely and bored children can bond.

Come to think of it, sometimes I wondered if I would have been just as attached to her if she'd been a dog.

Shaking my head, I turned around again and gestured at my face.

"Seriously, Sam. Look at me. I look like I spent all night rolling around in a grave. I can't remember anything that happened after supper last night. I know it sounds completely crazy, but I think I'm dead."

"I don't know what to say, Alex. Maybe you're just coming down with something?" Sam grimaced at my disbelieving look. "Okay, I admit, you do kinda look dead."

Sam shrugged helplessly, scrunching her nose up. She was wiggling it to push up her glasses again. I tried not to say anything, but I'd always found that particular move of hers irritating. It wasn't like I was much better. I had glasses too, although I preferred the more subtle look to her giant 'look-at-me' glasses.

Personally, I didn't think either of us had the face for glasses, but we also both shared the common torture of allergies, so contacts weren't something either of us attempted, unless we were trying to impress someone.

Probably a good thing, since when I'd looked at my eyes a second ago, they were bloodshot and kind of foggy looking. If I didn't know better, I'd say I was getting cataracts.

I glared at myself as a trickle of unease slid down my spine.

Suddenly, her eyes went as big as saucers and she leaned closer to examine me more carefully. "Maybe you really are dead!"

She turned her head as she looked me over, going from one ear to the other, looking me up and down from head to toe. I tried not to flinch.

"Your clothes are certainly dirty enough," she mused, walking around to examine me from the back. When she returned to face me and caught my eye, she nodded grimly. "I think you're right. I think you might be dead."

I groaned, then covered my mouth with surprise. We looked at each other, our eyes wide, as what emitted from my mouth sounded suspiciously like every zombie movie we'd watched in the last year.

We were both comfortable admitting we were super zombie nerds. We'd spent many hours, on many weekends, watching every single zombie movie we could get our hands on. The majority were so incredibly cheesy we spent most of our time laughing and throwing popcorn at the TV, while others gave us just the perfect amount of thrills.

One of the things we'd always made the most fun of was the way they sounded. Now we looked at each other and burst out laughing at the stereotypical zombie noise which had filled the air between us. My laughter may have had an edge of hysteria, but I felt it was justified under the circumstances.

"Okay, so if I'm dead, shouldn't I be craving, like, you know, like—"

Sam finished my sentence the way she often did. "—brains."

I nodded. "Exactly. Shouldn't I be, like, hungry for brains?"

Sam shrugged. "I don't know. Maybe the movies are wrong?"

I raised my eyebrows and groaned again, causing us both to snicker.

"Okay, fine," Sam held up her hand. "So the groaning thing appears to have been right, at least."

I began to pace around the bedroom. After a few steps it struck me that even my gait was stiffer than usual, and could be best described as an odd, stumbling lurch. I flung my head back and stopped dead.

"Oh, come on. This is ridiculous. Is it just me or did I look like I was moving like a zombie just now?"

Sam nodded, wrinkling her nose again as her glasses shimmied back up.

"Well, shit."

She was sitting on the edge of my bed, nodding her head as she templed her fingers and tapped them together. We didn't speak for a minute, both of us trying to figure out what the hell was going on. I kept coming back to one idea. Everything had been totally normal until supper last night.

I remembered coming home from school, putting my backpack in my room, then going downstairs to immediately eat the lasagna my mom had made for supper. I knew I'd eaten early because I'd dropped my lunch at school and had been starving.

Things had been totally normal until after I'd gotten off the phone with Sam—we'd been watching tv together and texting from our respective rooms, both of us too lazy to decide if we wanted to leave our houses. The last thing I recalled was feeling like maybe I had food poisoning and telling my mom I was going to lie down.

That was it.

When I got to the bathroom this morning and saw my reflection in the mirror, I'd let out a scream loud enough to wake the dearly departed and immediately texted Sam to come over.

Which was why were in my room at eight a.m. on Saturday morning, October 31, and we were both pretty sure I was a zombie.

Sam finally looked up from her mad scientist hands with an apologetic look on her face. "I think we have to face the facts, Alex. I think your mom killed you last night."

I shook my head, not wanting to believe she was right, even though I had the same suspicion. "But why? I mean, she's not the greatest cook in the world, but I made it to sixteen eating her food. Surely a vegetarian lasagna couldn't kill me!"

Sam shrugged, raising her left shoulder almost to her ear as she tilted her head.

"All I can say is that you appear zombie-like, based on our extensive research of zombie movies, good and bad. But, like, a fresh zombie. None of your parts look like they're falling off yet, so that's good, right?" Her voice squeaked a little at the end, making the question less than reassuring.

I knew she was trying to make me feel better. But as always, when Sam was trying to be helpful, I was left feeling vaguely irritated instead.

"It's not working!" I was practically shouting now and immediately felt bad at the chastened look on her face.

"I'm sorry," she said quietly, her head slumping onto her chest.

I sat next to her on the other side of my bed, patting her back. "I know, you're trying to be helpful. But look at me! How the heck am I going to get Zach to ask me out looking like this?"

Once again, I gestured furiously at my face with my hands. The blue discoloration of my fingernails caught my attention and I groaned again. We giggled, but mine still had a nervous edge to it.

I wasn't sure I liked the noises I was making, no matter how into zombie movies I was.

My normally blue eyes had a grayish tint to them when I'd seen them in the mirror, which matched my skin nicely, and I turned them to Sam to stare at her with as much sorrow as I could muster.

Which, given how blue my eyes were, I suspected was a fair amount.

"What if I try to eat you? That's an awful way to lose your best friend."

There. I'd said it.

Her eyes went wide for a moment as she processed my words, before she narrowed them. "You're not acting like a typical zombie so far."

She tapped her mouth with her index finger. I could almost see the thoughts percolating through her head. This was one of the reasons I loved her so much. Whenever I was stuck, she stepped up.

Her eyes lit up, and she pointed her finger at me. "Wait a minute, you said your mom gave you a vegetarian lasagna last night?"

I nodded slowly, not sure where she was going with her train of thought. I gasped. "Wait a minute, are you saying..."

"Maybe you're a vegetarian zombie."

We both leapt off the bed with excitement.

"You still think I'm really dead though?"

I didn't want to be dead. Not for real, anyway. I had stuff to do with my life. Stuff which wouldn't be possible for a dead girl. Or a lot harder at least.

She grabbed my wrist and held it for a second while she concentrated, then dropped it, nodding emphatically. "No pulse. You're def dead."

Instead of being nervous about the potential of me eating her, Sam appeared inappropriately excited. This time, I was the one backing up.

"I'm not sure I like the look on your face right now." I backed up another step.

She continued to approach, looking at me like I was a bug under glass. "Think about it, Alex. What if you *are* a vegetarian zombie? We've never seen a movie about one of those. Maybe you have, like, cool powers or something."

I shook my head, backing up until I bumped against the wall, then nervously searched for an escape route to either side.

She was watching me with too much interest for my comfort. I suddenly had an inkling of how people with powers felt when 'the man' wanted to experiment on them.

"I don't know, Sam. Zombies seem pretty dumb in general, and they don't have any powers other than being able to keep moving after body parts fall off."

Sam looked deflated at my logical answer, but it was only temporary. She snapped her fingers as an idea hit her. "True," she started, pointing at me again. "But you don't sound dumb. You sound just like you always do."

"Wait, is that good or bad?"

It was too early for me to be grasping what she was trying to say. Or maybe my brain was atrophying as we spoke.

She rolled her eyes, giving me a sly grin. "Don't worry. I'll keep your zombie secret. The same way I kept your math test secret."

I gave her a baleful glare at the attempt at humor but was glad to see she'd stopped trying to pin me to the wall. She turned her attention to my bedroom door and was almost at the handle when I stopped her.

"Wait a minute, where are you going?"

She gave me a reassuring smile. "I want to check out the kitchen and see what's in the fridge."

My mouth dropped open with surprise and as I went to close it, my tongue hit my back right molar. Huh, it felt loose. I put my finger in the back of my mouth and gave it a wiggle. It came out easily. I looked down at the tooth in disbelief.

Sam bit her lip. "I'm thinking maybe we should figure out what's going on, quickly." She was looking at my tooth with concern before meeting my eyes. "If your teeth are loose already, I'm not sure how much time we have."

Cradling my tooth in my hand, I followed her down the stairs as a numb sensation spread through me. I wasn't sure if it was shock, or worse. I took the stairs carefully, just in case. I wasn't graceful while alive and didn't want to chance falling while dead.

"I'd probably lose an arm or leg if I did that," I muttered.

"What did you say?" Sam turned around, pausing on the bottom stair.

I shook my head. "Nothing."

She gave me a suspicious look, then shrugged, stepping into the foyer ahead of me. We tiptoed into the kitchen, but it wasn't necessary. I could tell from the lack of action no one else was awake yet. They must have been out late the night before.

In fact, I think my mom had said she was going out shortly after I started to feel sick.

"Sam," I hissed, causing her to turn around.

She gave me an odd look. "Alex," she hissed back, before resuming a normal volume. "Why are you whispering?"

I stopped, squinted in an attempt to focus my eyes, and realized she was right. Why *was* I whispering? I was in my own house at eight o'clock on a Saturday morning. It was completely normal for me to be in the kitchen at that time of day with Sam, hanging out.

I shrugged, giving her an 'I don't know' look. "Sorry. Obviously, I'm not quite myself today."

We looked at each other and began snickering as we thought about how true that sentence was. Once we'd collected ourselves, Sam turned to open the fridge. I waited as she stuck her hand in and rummaged around on the shelves.

In a flurry of activity, she began to pull items out and place them on the counter. One was the lasagna, but she kept loading up the counter with stuff I hadn't eaten in days until it was completely covered.

"What are you doing?"

She shut the fridge, winking at me over her shoulder. "Like you said. If you're a zombie, you should be hungry, right?"

She stepped back to show me what she'd placed on the counter. In the time she'd had her head in the fridge, she'd managed to pull out not only the lasagna, but some raw hamburger meat that mom had thawing, a head of lettuce, and a piece of pizza along with a variety of mystery containers. My lip curled back as I looked at them.

"That's an interesting combination."

I nodded my head as though speaking with somebody very slow. Or perhaps, someone speaking a different language. She was my best friend, but I hardly ever understood the way her brain worked.

She gestured for me to stand in front of her, next to the food. "Okay, tell me. When you look at these, which one makes you feel the hungriest right now."

I raised my eyebrow as she shooed me forward.

"Go on, take a big sniff of everything then tell me what you want. One of these things has got to make you feel a little bit grumbly in the tumbly."

I rolled my eyes. Knowing Sam, if I didn't humor her she'd just keep nagging. I stood in front of the items, staring at each in turn before soulfully looking back at her.

"Nothing. Now what?"

She rolled her eyes at me. "Come on, Alex. I want you to smell them, maybe even touch them a little bit. You know, jiggle something inside that fresh zombie brain of yours."

This time I glared but did what she'd asked. I leaned over, taking a deep inhale from each object. The lasagna smelled surprisingly good, considering I'm pretty sure it had killed me. Shaking my head, I moved on to the next item, the hamburger meat. I have to admit I was a little bit nervous about this one, since it was so close to people food. If people counted as food.

To my surprise, when I took a deep whiff of the meat I felt as though I was going to vomit. I covered my mouth and backed up.

"Oh, gross!" I spoke from behind my hand while pushing it away with the other, giving her a disgusted look.

A big smile split her face. "Keep going. The other things."

I sighed, turning back to the remaining items. The pizza and the head of lettuce.

The lettuce was closest, and I leaned in toward it. I wasn't sure if lettuce even had a smell, but when I was a few inches away, my eyes and mouth began to water. A wave of hunger spread through me and to my shock and dismay, I lost control.

I watched my hand grab the lettuce and shove the entire head into my mouth. My eyeballs rolled up and I moaned in ecstasy as I chewed. Pieces of green splattered all over my chest and rained down on to the floor. Once the lettuce was finished, sanity returned, and as it did, I looked at Sam with horror.

She was still smiling but now also appeared a little grossed out.

"Two things," she said, holding up her index and middle finger on her right hand. "One, I'm really happy you didn't do that with the hamburger meat. And two, that was super nasty. Try not to do that in front of me again, mmkay?"

I nodded my head dumbly, brushing lettuce pieces off my chest as I attempted to process what had just happened. "I fed like a zombie from the movies, didn't I."

Sam nodded. "Yep, you sure did. Now, take a sniff of the pizza. Not that I expect much. I'm pretty sure we've already got our answer."

I turned back to smell the pizza, wrinkling my nose as I pushed it away. While not as gross as the hamburger meat had been, it didn't appeal in the slightest. I turned to face Sam, wiping my mouth as I collected my thoughts.

"I'm a teenage vegetarian zombie, aren't I?"

Sam nodded with satisfaction. "Yes, I believe you are."

Chapter 2

Sam had gone home, leaving shortly after our little adventure in the kitchen. She said she needed to look something up and take a shower. I hadn't objected, for the simple reason I was pretty sure I also needed a shower.

Far more than she did.

I'd showered the day before, but apparently being dead made me feel a little less-than-fresh and I was self-conscious about possibly smelling deceased. Not to mention, I still thought it looked like I'd found garbage to roll around in at some point during the night.

I didn't usually wear perfume or makeup, but after giving myself another critical once-over in the bathroom mirror, I decided today was the perfect day to start. I may have also been motivated by the fact it was actually Halloween and we were supposed to go over to Zach's for the party tonight.

I shrugged. I may as well spend the day in character. So, instead of putting on foundation to hide my pale skin, I added dark eyeliner to highlight it, leaving the now pasty and slightly gray skin obvious for the world to see. If I'd complained I was pale in the past, my current complexion resembled day-old mashed potatoes now.

Luckily, it complemented the dark circles under my eyes beautifully.

Slipping my wire frame glasses onto my face, I took a last pass at myself in the mirror. I looked pretty much the same as usual otherwise, except for the fact I was already down one tooth. Thankfully it was a back tooth. I was suspicious my left ear was hanging lower than usual as well, but hopefully it would stay in place until after the party.

The last thing I wanted while trying to get Zach to notice me was have an ear fall off. Pretty sure that's right up there in the top five on the list of things *not* to do to impress a boy.

Wrapping the towel tightly around my chest, I padded back to my bedroom, shutting the door without encountering anyone on the way. I looked at the clock on my alarm, frowning when I saw it was after nine. I still hadn't heard anyone else moving inside the house.

"That's not normal," I muttered. Usually at least one of my parents was up by now. Then again, what exactly had been normal today?

Sighing, I looked through my closet. What should I wear? Hmmm, jeans, jeans, more jeans, t-shirts, hoodies. I bit my lip, stopping when I felt it move more than it should have.

"Nope. If you want any chance with Zach, you're going to need to have both lips firmly attached." I frowned at myself in my dresser mirror and decided I needed a pep talk. "Just remember; you're smart enough, good enough, and doggone it, you don't eat people's brains."

I snorted at my lame attempt at humor then looked back at the closet. Oh yeah. I'd almost forgotten about that outfit. Before I had a chance to change my mind, I yanked out the super short skirt I'd been meaning to wear for several months. I'd never had the courage before, but with everything else going on, it seemed far less frightening now.

"After all, I can't die of embarrassment." I put the skirt on and gave myself a critical once-over in the mirror.

I looked okay, actually.

Maybe even more than okay. I checked out my backside. The skirt was a red and black plaid schoolgirl cut, barely enough to cover my butt. It wasn't the kind of thing I could wear to school, but Halloween was the one night in the year when you could go as you weren't.

In this case, as a hooker.

And alive.

I examined my face one last time, feeling glum again. Normally when I looked at the mirror for blemishes, I was thinking pimples and whiteheads. Blemishes took on a whole new meaning today as I looked for any areas that might be peeling off.

So far, so good. I shook my head and slowly backed away from the mirror. I'd spent enough time on my appearance already. It was time to figure out where my parents were.

I left my bedroom, listening for any noise to tell me where they were as I walked. Hearing nothing, I continued on to their bedroom and tapped on the door quietly.

"Mom? Dad? Are you sleeping?"

After a minute, when there was no answer, I took a deep breath and put my hand on the doorknob. Half expecting it to be locked, I jiggled it.

It turned easily underneath my hand.

"Okay, this is getting strange."

I opened the door slowly, part of me hoping I was about to walk in on something I didn't want to see just so long as I found them here. As I allowed the door to creak open slowly and looked around, the feeling I'd been fighting back all morning washed over me.

They weren't home.

The breath I'd taken in for courage escaped in a gust of disappointment, and I inhaled a growing sense of unease. I walked all the way through their bedroom to peek in the en-suite, just in case, but they weren't there, either.

Pursing my lips while reminding myself not to bite my cheeks, I looked through each upstairs room before going back downstairs. I walked into the kitchen, then passed through to the dining, living room, and office.

Nothing. No one else was in the house. Patting my pocket, I realized I'd left my cell phone in my bedroom. I carefully stomped upstairs to retrieve it and immediately texted both of my parents. When they didn't answer, I texted Sam.

I waited impatiently for someone to respond. It felt like forever, but in actuality, it was only five minutes. At first I was excited, thinking it was my mom or dad, but when I saw it was Sam, I jumped right into my concerns.

Hey.

Hey. What's up?

I can't find my parents. :-(

:-o No way!

Yes way. I looked everywhere.

Do you think they would've gone somewhere without telling you?

Not them. Unless they've been replaced by aliens, or something.

: (It could be possible. I mean, example, you.

Not helping. Can you help me come look for them?

Sure. Where do you want to go?

Not sure. It's Saturday. Maybe we can drive around town, look around? Can you borrow the car?

Maybe. Let me check.

(...)

I waited as the three little dots hovered on the screen, and not for the first time, thought about how irritating they were. I'd much rather just wait for someone to reply instead of seeing those little dots taunting me.

Okay. Come over. Dad said I can take it for two hours but need to be back at noon.

Okay. BRT

I got my coat and keys, pausing at the front door. Today had already been the absolute strangest day of my life, and I wasn't looking forward to more surprises. But the fact that I didn't know where my parents were worried me even more than the fact I was technically dead.

I scratched the back of my neck absently, grimacing when a small chunk of flesh came away under my fingernail. I smoothed it down and pushed my long hair over it. At this point, I was hoping I stayed in one piece long enough to find my parents and get to the party tonight.

Apparently, this Halloween could be my last.

Chapter 3

Thankfully, Sam was a good driver. I carefully buckled in, not because I was worried about safety, but because I was fast becoming concerned that any abrupt movement could cause me to lose a body part.

Or two.

She turned, left hand on the steering wheel, her right elbow on the center console and gave me a look. "Okay, so where to? Where do you think your parents would be if they're not home on a Saturday morning?"

I raised my arm helplessly. "That's the problem. This has never happened before. I mean, I'm sixteen, and not knowing where they are is freaking me out even more than finding out I'm a zombie. My parents would never, I repeat, *never*, leave without telling me where they were going."

Sam wrinkled her nose, absently pushing up her glasses. "Is it possible they did say something, but it was around the time you went to bed and you just don't remember?"

I shrugged. "I don't know. That whole evening was just..." I shook my head. "Weird. Seriously, the last thing I remember was the lasagna and heading to bed. I think my mom said she was going out, but it's all fuzzy."

I concentrated hard on the memory, remembering the delicious way the lasagna had slid down my throat. At the time, I recall thinking she'd actually done a good job for once when it came to making something pleasant outside of a box...wait a minute.

I turned to Sam, excitement bubbling up. At least I was hoping it was excitement, not my stomach. "What if my mom didn't make the lasagna?"

Her eyebrows lifted. "What do you mean?"

I leaned forward, a faint idea percolating through my slowly stiffening thought processes.

"I remember thinking my mom had done a strangely good job on the lasagna." I raised my eyebrows. "You know how stellar her cooking is."

She rolled her eyes. "Oh, yeah. I've been subjected to her skills more than once over the years. Just remember, I'm still waiting for my best friend medal for never saying anything to her."

I nodded. "I know. That's one of the reasons she lets us hang out. But anyway. She said she made the lasagna. What if she actually bought it?"

Sam's eyes went wide the second she got where I was going with my line of thinking. "Wait— do you think it was from the new catering place in town?"

I nodded slowly, careful not to knock anything loose. "It could be. That may explain why they aren't home."

Sam looked confused again. "Well, where would your parents be if they're not at home that has something to do with the catering company? You can't eat there."

"True," I agreed. "But that doesn't mean they didn't go somewhere the new place catered for yesterday evening."

"Well, that could explain things." Her eyes went wide again as the next logical idea struck her. "Do you think they could be..."

"Zombies?" I winced. "Yeah, it's crossed my mind."

Frowning, she turned the corner heading into the downtown. "What would be the purpose? I mean, why would anybody want to make people into zombies?"

I shook my head carefully again. "Beats the heck out of me. We should think about some of the movies we've watched. We might get some ideas."

She regarded me skeptically. "Yeah, but those are all movies. Not real life."

I gestured to my body. "We thought zombies were pretend until this morning too."

She sighed. "Yeah, good point. Okay then, first off, Chaos Catering. Hey." She stopped at a stop sign and her eyebrows went up. "That's a fitting title for the company, assuming they did this to you, of course."

I nodded slowly. "Yeah, that's kind of what made me think of them in the first place."

We didn't talk much after that, with Sam needing to concentrate on the heavier than usual Saturday morning traffic and while I thought about how my life had spun out of control. It had always been dangerous to eat my mom's cooking, but not like this.

This was ridiculous.

The car stopped and I saw we were parked on the street beside the new catering store. It was a regular strip-mall in a small town. Nothing about the place stood out in any way. Even the sign itself was rather boring; big block letters in a dark color not quite dark enough to be a legit black. If it had been up to me, I probably would've put up some decorations or something.

It looked more like an accountant's office than a catering company.

I waited for Sam to open her door then I got out as well.

"Should we try to go in?" Her whisper was loud in my ear.

I glared, unimpressed not surprised by her lack of subtlety. The blue glasses were a dead giveaway to what kind of personality she had. Sam was about as subtle as a sledgehammer, which provided a good balance to my usual shyness.

"The sign says it's open. We can go in, see if they have any food for sale, and maybe pick up a brochure or something."

She wrinkled her nose skeptically. "You think we'll find anything? I mean, I highly doubt they'll have the zombie-making lasagna in the front with a big sign."

I rolled my eyes but quickly stopped, closing them against a sudden, sharp pain. That hadn't felt very good. I think some of the muscles in my eyes were getting loose. I added another motion to the list of things which weren't safe for me to perform as a zombie. So far, this one had hurt more than the others.

As I'd always loved a good eye roll in lieu of sarcasm, I felt the loss deeply.

"We won't know unless we look," I finally managed, earning a shrug in return.

"Sure. Whatever you say." She gave me a quick once over, noticed the way I was squinting, and reached for the door. "Here, maybe let me do most things for a bit. Just until we figure this out."

I nodded glumly and walked inside.

Chapter 4

While the outside looked like an office, the inside was clearly a place that sold food. Lots of food. There were bays of freezers, as well as dried goods on shelves and countertops. At any other time, I probably would've been hungry looking at the variety. But with my new, zombie-vegetarian taste preferences, the presence of the non-vegetable selections turned my stomach.

I took a deep breath and was overwhelmed by the odors surrounding me. I turned away from the fresh food selection, telling my stomach to stay put. When I did, I noticed something strange. While we had been correct there wasn't seating like in a restaurant or cafe, I caught a glimpse of a large table through an open door to the back room.

"Hey, Sam."

She whipped her head around in the direction I was pointing and tilted it, appearing oddly similar to a bloodhound on a trail as she did.

Clearly, she found the back as interesting as I did.

"Should we look? I don't see anyone around."

She was right. Other than the two of us, no one else seemed to be in the building. Very strange. There should have been at least one person manning the counter, but even with the dingle of the doorbell, no one had come out to the front to greet potential customers.

I slowly followed her as she crept in an exaggerated tip-toe to the back. Part of this was the fact I was naturally more cautious than she was, but also because my knees didn't seem to want to bend all the way anymore.

Things were moving quickly. I was beginning to get worried I'd never see my parents, or Zach, again.

The back room was as empty of people as the display area in the front, so we cautiously continued forward and began to rifle through the papers and supplies.

Nothing seemed out of place.

"I'm not seeing much. Does anything jump out at you?"

"No," I replied glumly, putting my hand to my throat at the sound which emerged.

Her eyebrows shot up. "We better work faster. When you said that, you sounded just like Ghoulia from *Monster High.*"

I sighed. "I know. My joints are starting to stiffen up too."

She gave me a sympathetic look as she gently patted my back. "We'll find out what's going on and reverse it. I guarantee it."

She looked around, and a smile spread over her face at the sight of fresh chopped vegetables. "Here, maybe you just need some energy. Why don't you try these?"

"What are they?" I said, looking at the greens as I slurped back my spit. My mouth was starting to water an embarrassing amount.

"Well, I'm pretty sure these are artichoke hearts, and those are brussel sprouts." She gave me a funny look. "You've never seen brussel sprouts before?"

I shrugged. "No, I've seen them before, it's just..." I pointed at my eyes, feeling ashamed. "I think I've got cataracts."

She frowned. "Damn. Here, eat up."

I accepted the vegetables and once again, my hunger temporarily overwhelmed me. Ignoring everything around me, I chowed down. Once they were gone, I realized she'd been right.

I did feel a bit better.

"Hey, thanks! I can see now. And I'm a little less stiff." I looked around, spying celery and asparagus on the table a little further away. I took them, putting them in my hoodie pocket for later. I wasn't hungry at the moment, but I may need them again soon at the rate I was decomposing.

"Duh-duh-duh-duh. *Duh-duh-duh-duh.*" I snickered when Sam gave me a look. "What? Just thinking of Mozart and how we're the same."

She tilted her head. "Did I miss something? Are your synapses skipping the tracks?"

I pushed up my glasses and grinned. "No, man. We're both decomposing."

This time, Sam was the one who groaned.

I kept loading my pockets as I snorted at my own joke and once finished, I took another look around. My eyes weren't as foggy, and now that I could see better, I noticed the back door into the alley was standing about a foot open.

"Huh, that's weird."

"What is?" She looked at me with confusion.

I pointed to the back, partially blocked by a large freezer. "The door to the alley is open."

"That's interesting. I wonder if somebody left just before we got here?"

I shrugged, noticed my shoulders felt slightly better than when we'd entered. Apparently, veggies did a body good. I took a celery stalk out of my pocket and nibbled on it while I thought.

My eyes zoomed in on a speck of green on the ground, just outside the doorway. I cautiously bent over, putting my left hand on my lower back like I was a hundred and used the other to pick up the item. When I showed Sam, she made a humming sound.

"What is it?" She came to stand beside me, pushing her glasses up as she squinted for a better look.

"If I'm not mistaken, it's a piece of romaine." Without thinking, I popped the piece of evidence into my mouth. "Yup, def romaine."

"Alex! What if that was evidence?"

I grimaced. "Sorry, I don't seem to have much control when it comes to vegetables. Kind of ironic really, considering it took ten years or so until my parents could convince me to eat anything other than peas and carrots."

She nodded agreeably. "True. They'd never believe it if they could see you..." she trailed off lamely as the reason we were there returned.

I shook my head. "It's okay. Let's see what's out back. Maybe we'll find more clues in the alley."

Sam pushed the door open. "Yeah, I don't see anything inside that tells us much."

She let me go first again but just like the building, the alley was deserted and completely empty except a single, large dumpster. I looked at the dumpster, then at Sam, giving her a slow smile.

She lowered her chin and stuck out her lower lip. "Are you serious?" She pointed at the dumpster, then to herself. "You want me to go in there?"

I winked. "Yeah, I may be dead, but at least your parts aren't starting to fall off. We may as well both smell the same."

Sam rolled her eyes but didn't argue. I was certain she was thinking how fast I'd been moving and couldn't deny the risk I'd fall in and be unable to get out. Spotting an overturned box next to the dumpster, she used it to launch herself into the bin.

I was impressed.

It had been a few years since the last time she'd done anything athletic. Apparently, the couple years of tumbling she'd done in middle school had stuck with her. I made a mental note to see if she could still walk on her hands.

Maybe she could try at the party tonight, distract everyone from my hands falling off.

I waited as she rustled around inside for a few minutes before she finally popped her head up over the edge.

"Well, I think I know where you got to last night."

I tilted my head. "What you mean?"

She held my watch up triumphantly and tossed it to me.

I caught it reflexively, fumbling and almost dropping it when my reflexes turned out to be way slower than I remembered. It definitely was my watch, but how? I checked my wrist, shocked to realize I hadn't been wearing it and doubly shocked I hadn't noticed it missing before now.

How had I not noticed?

Sam smiled down at me, resting her head on her crossed arms at the lip of the dumpster. "You always did say you'd have to be dead to take it off."

I nodded absently. I had said that, multiple times. I'd always felt naked without wearing a watch, practically since learning to tell time, yet hadn't even realized it was gone. As I thought back over my morning though, I thought I understood why.

I'd been far too alarmed and overwhelmed at discovering I was dead to give my faithful time-teller any consideration.

But how had it ended up in the dumpster in the first place?

Putting it on, I looked at Sam. "Thanks. Did you see anything else in there?"

"I'm not sure. Give me a sec." She ducked back into the dumpster.

More noises emitted, including several suggesting the first thing she planned to do when she got out was have a shower. A moment later, she popped her head up again.

"There seems to be a fair amount of moldy vegetables in here, and..." She bit her lip, looking down, then back at me with a pained expression on her face.

As the pause stretched on longer than I could handle, I prompted her. "What?"

She winced. "I don't think you're gonna like this. I've found more of what looks like the lasagna you had at home. There seems to be a few batches in here. Like, a lot." She gave me an apologetic look. "Maybe they found out that it was a bad batch. Maybe the lasagna you ate last night was from here?"

I scoffed. "As if! No way would my mom ever go dumpster diving to get me supper."

She shook her head. "That's not what I mean. What if your mom bought the lasagna last night from the batch that's in here? Maybe they didn't know it was bad until..."

I nodded slowly, her meaning sinking in. "Until someone died."

Sam shook her head slowly and her eyes locked onto mine. "Do you think it's the kind of secret someone would kill over?"

As I mulled over her question, I couldn't help thinking she might be onto something. "If the lasagna was bad, who else ate it before they found out? And why are my parents missing?"

As she shrugged, an idea began to form in my head. I concentrated hard on her pensive expression and it came to me.

"Wait a minute. What if after I ate the lasagna, my mom did something when I said I wasn't feeling good?"

Sam's eyes went wide. "Would she have gone back to the caterer? Is that the kind of thing she'd do?"

As we looked at each other, we both knew the answer.

"Who are we trying to kid? Of course she would've gone back. You know how she is when she thinks she's gotten a bad deal on something or if her food wasn't done exactly how she wanted it to be at a restaurant?"

She nodded. "So if she thought you'd gotten sick right after eating the lasagna..."

"... she went back to the caterers to complain." I bit my lip, instantly regretting it as a piece of tissue gave way.

Sam apparently thought it was funny. "OMG, Alex. Your lip just ballooned right up. It, like, doubled in size!"

I gently touched the area I'd bit, closing my eyes with mortification. She was right. I couldn't see what it looked like, but it was definitely abnormal as I felt along the upper limits of the vermilion border.

Maybe I could make it work for me. We were living in the age of collagen fillers after all. I could make it part of the whole

Halloween thing. At least with the rate I was falling apart it was unlikely I'd have to worry about what I looked like at school on Monday.

"The thing that bothers me most is *both* your parents are missing." Sam leaned over the edge of the dumpster, looking like she was going to fall out. "Why wouldn't one of them have stayed home with you if you were sick?"

I groaned as another chunk of memory fell back into place. "Oh, man. I'm not sure why I didn't remember before."

Sam began tapping on the side of the dumpster, a dull ting-ting punctuating her words. "Remember what?"

I shook my head, stopping when a piece of hair fell off. I looked at her, wondering if she'd noticed. She had, but didn't comment. "My dad wasn't home yesterday. He's on rotation at the airport."

"So when you tried to text him earlier..."

"He was probably still sleeping or on the plane."

I was relieved to know the whereabouts of at least one of my parents, which reminded me. Pulling out my cell phone, I sent him a text. Disappointed he hadn't responded to the earlier ones, I reassured myself it had only been a few hours. If he was in the air it wasn't unusual for him to take a while to reply.

Plus, what was I going to say to explain what was going on even if he did get back to me? Mom was missing, and I was a zombie who had ethical issues with meat?

I looked at Sam once I'd finished texting. "Okay, so the good news is we aren't looking for both my parents, just–"

"—your mom." She gestured inside the dumpster. "Let me take one more look."

I waited as she sifted through the garbage. This time when she stood up, her face was white. I knew she'd found something totally awful even before she held up the cell phone.

It wasn't just any cell phone. The lock screen had a picture I was well acquainted with. My heart sank, creating a dull sloshing feeling inside as the full realization this was actually happening landed like a stone in my gut.

I was looking at a Halloween picture of me, my mom, and my dad from last year. Every year around the holidays, my mom either got a new picture or used the one from the year before. She said it was a way to keep her in the 'the holiday spirit', but I'd always thought it was a little cheesy.

Looking at the picture now though, tears stung my eyes.

Like, actually stung.

"Ouch." I carefully patted the moisture under my eyelids, pulling my lip back in disgust when I saw my hands. "Ewww, gross. Note to self, no more crying."

I caught a similar look on Sam's face before she managed to hide it. "Yeah, let's not have you do that anymore, okay?"

Instead of tears, we'd both been unpleasantly treated to the sight of black goo sliding down my cheeks. I wasn't sure if it was what happened when you were dead, or if it was some weird byproduct of my new vegetarian lifestyle. Either way, I was happy to never experience it again.

"Come to think of it, you look kinda cute," she said, with far too much false cheer. "Instant smoky eyes!"

I glared. "Thanks. Pass the phone. I'll see if there's anything on it."

This time instead of tossing it, having witnessed my near miss with the watch, she put it in her back pocket and laboriously climbed out of the dumpster. Once back on the ground, she handed it over.

And that was when I discovered something I hadn't expected to see.

Chapter 5

Okay. I freely admit I probably shouldn't know how to get into my mom's phone. After all, there was a reason she'd password protected it in the first place, although it wasn't because of me, I promise.

Either way, she had a pretty easy password. My birthday, of course. She was a great mom, just an awful cook. I knew she loved me, which was why I'd panicked when I couldn't find either of my parents this morning.

I was used to my dad being away. He frequently left me with my mom for his work as a pilot with a major airline, but she'd always been a constant. That was probably why what I found on her phone shocked me so much.

After I waltzed past the lock screen, the first thing I checked were her messages. Several came from a number I didn't recognize and made me wonder exactly what had been going on. She hadn't entered the contact name, so all I could see was the other number. I screenshot it with my own phone, in case it ended up being important.

The conversation started out fairly ordinary, but I could see it had been going on for well over a week. It looked as though my mom had been planning some sort of a Halloween party. But for whom? I didn't remember her saying anything. I wasn't going to be home tonight, so I knew it wasn't for me. I'd been talking non-stop about Zach's party for the past three weeks so she wouldn't have planned a surprise that would have ruined that.

"Sam, look at these." I showed her the messages.

As she read, her face twisted into the same confusion I felt. "Wait, your mom is planning a party?"

I frowned. "It looks like it, but it's the first I've heard of it."

What were the chances there was more than one Halloween party tonight? We lived in a small town of about five thousand people, about a half an hour outside of Calgary. It was a pretty regular town. A lot of people worked in the city and came home in the evening, like my dad. It was certainly possible to have more than one party on the same night, especially on Halloween, but hard to believe I hadn't known about it.

Why hadn't I known about it?

The party I was going to was being held at Zach's and was for high school kids only. So, my mom could have been organizing or going to a Halloween party somewhere else for adults, but she had no reason to hide it from me. At least, none I knew of.

"Do you think this number belongs to the catering company?"

I hoped Sam had some ideas, but her blank expression didn't give me confidence.

"I don't know what to think anymore. Looking at our timeline of events, it sounds like everything was normal yesterday. You came home and had supper with your mom and your dad is out of town."

I nodded, happy about that for a change, and she continued to list things, using her fingers for emphasis.

"You woke up dead today, and apparently vegetables are your crack." Sam raised her eyebrows. "Which is cool, otherwise it would be totally friends-off if you tried to eat my brains. And now your mom is missing, presumed to have at some point gone dumpster-diving, possibly in the same dumpster you enjoy frequenting."

Despite myself, a laugh escaped. One thing Sam was really good at was making me laugh, even when things seemed to be at their darkest

"Yeah. I ate the lasagna and felt sick, so I went to bed early. At some point, I remember my mom peeking her head in and saying she was going to go out. When I woke up this morning, I was dirty all over and had no pulse, which you verified when I called you. My mom wasn't home, and my dad is out of town working, I hope. I don't remember going anywhere last night though, so I can neither confirm nor deny I was in the dumpster, or how I would have gotten there and back. "

I silently admitted to myself there was a possibility my dad could be missing too, although it was less likely now that I'd remembered he'd left for work Friday morning.

"If your mom was organizing a Halloween party for tonight with the same catering company she bought the lasagna from and she went back to complain about you getting sick, what if she canceled her order? Or maybe she walked in on something they were trying to hide, such as, oh I don't know, dead bodies or bad food?"

Her eyes were shining behind her oversized glasses with a little too much glee at the idea of more dead bodies.

"Maybe."

I was confused by everything that was happening, but couldn't be sure if it was because my brain was slowing down, or if it was because nothing about anything made sense anymore. I really hoped it was because nothing made sense, otherwise, I wasn't even going to make it to the party tonight.

I took another celery stalk out of my pocket and munched on it, feeling a little brighter as I did. An idea came to me as I finished crunching.

"Wait a minute, I read this number because it stuck out as weird, but what if there's messages from other people? Maybe they can point us to what's going on."

Sam gestured at the phone. "Okay, who else was your mom texting last night?"

Quickly, I scrolled through her other messages, ignoring the ones I'd sent this morning. Apparently while I was dying last night, I hadn't bothered to contact her. The last text prior to this morning was one from her bestie, Tracy. I honed in on it, swallowing hard as I read.

Where are you?

I'm here, where are you?

I'll be there in ten

Tracy's last three messages hadn't been answered, but the one right before them was interesting. My mom had given her friend an address, along with what might be a cryptic warning.

1313 Baycrest close.

I think there's something big going on.

Heading there now.

Get here ASAP.

The phone drifted down as I looked at Sam. I wondered if my face had paled further from its already dead fish-belly white complexion.

Sam had been reading along with me and looked as concerned as I felt. "You don't think she went there, do you?"

My face must've convinced her I did, because she closed her eyes briefly.

"I really don't want to go there. We don't have to, right?" She gave me a beseeching look.

I patted her back, shaking my head. "Thanks, Sam. You've been a great friend. Hopefully, you can find another best friend without too much problem. I'm not sure I have much longer."

It was entirely a guilt trip and completely fatalistic, but she took the bait.

"Don't talk like that! We'll find something. Maybe there's an antidote. Sometimes there's antidotes, right? I mean, wasn't there that one episode of *Supernatural* where they turn somebody human?"

I shrugged weakly. "I'm pretty sure they changed a human back from a werewolf, and kept Dean from becoming a vamp once. But hey, if I can be a vegetarian zombie, who knows? Maybe there's one for that too. Stranger things have happened today." I held the phone up and turned back toward the building. "I have to go check this out. I mean, my mom could be in there. And maybe her friend too."

As the thought crossed my mind, I sent Tracy a quick text. We'd known each other for years and she was at our house almost as often as Sam. When no response came after a moment, I began to think adults didn't even check their phones.

"Fine. I'll go with you. If you think we have to, I won't bail on you. But just remember, I did this for you and your mom when I wind up dead too. I never wanted to go to that house again. I'm not sure I'd go there for my own mom," she added, looking glum.

I knew she what she was referring to. Once, on a dare a few years back, she'd rung the doorbell playing knock-on-ginger and almost had a heart attack when she'd been chased off the lawn. She tells it differently though. Personally, I think she'd built it up over the years and created her own horror movie out of it.

Exaggeration aside though, it was a super creepy house.

I bit off a chunk of asparagus for courage and swallowed it. "Thanks, but it's okay, really. Listen, it's already eleven. Why don't you drop me off and head home? I don't want you to get in trouble with your dad about the car. I'll be fine. I'm sure I can check it out on my own. After all, I'm already dead; what else can happen to me?"

Her face was the poster for color-me-insulted as she objected. "Hells, no! As if I'm letting my best friend go to the most creeptastic haunted house in town to be a zombie detective all by herself. No way, Jose. We're in this together."

I smiled weakly. I was happy to have her support but the reality of where we were going had fully sunk in as she spoke.

"I'm thinking I should grab some of the lasagna for the road. I have a bad feeling we may need it before this is over."

Chapter 6

We usually tried to stay away from this part of town.

It wasn't as though it was run-down or anything, but we'd heard stories over the years from other kids. People with pets who had gone missing, or a friend of a friends who had tried to trick-or-treat and narrowly escaped with their life.

The usual things you heard as a kid that made you believe in a boogeyman right before falling asleep. Nothing crazy, unless you listened to Sam's super exaggerated story, which I was trying hard to forget right now.

Something about the place we were heading to now made us believe the hype a bit more than the same stories told anywhere else. Maybe it had something to do with my newly undead status, or the fact my mom was missing. I was sure that played in somewhere.

When Sam pulled up a few houses away, it wasn't because there wasn't a closer parking space. It was one hundred percent due to our fear about who, or what, was inside.

The house we parked in front of was fine. It was a typical two story with pretty flowers in the front. Basically, it was a cookie-cutter, everyman house. The house two doors down with 1313 on the front was the one we dreaded.

I stared at it warily. It had 'Halloween' written all over it. It was hidden by thick, ancient trees, the oldest looking ones in town. I didn't know what kind they were, but they were dark and menacing and seemed to deliberately block the now almost midday sunlight from touching the ominous house behind it.

The house itself had been built so long ago people were still scared of getting hit by lightning. Every single one of the peaks had a wicked-sharp looking metal rod with a glass ball, reminding me of the mansions where mad scientists like Dr. Frankenstein worked.

Maybe if it had been a different color, or got a little more sunshine, it would've appeared different. Maybe it could have been as pretty as the other houses in the neighborhood.

Instead, every time I'd seen the house from up close, I'd been left with the vague impression something sinister lived inside.

I turned to see Sam watching it with a similar expression of foreboding. She grimaced, her hand hovering over the door handle to the car. "So...do we go?"

I groaned, sounding even more like Ghoulia. Our nervous laughter carried us out to the street and lasted until we were on the walk in front of the house.

The landscape wasn't well maintained. Leaves and branches were strewn all over the sidewalk, matted together, and made it difficult to see the cement in places. This in turn made me worry about the tripping hazard with my less-than-stellar balance at the best of times, let alone with corpse knees, which no longer bent normally.

It was impossible to tell just from the yard whether or not anybody had been living there. I noted only one rolled up newspaper on the doorstep, but it looked fresh instead of weathered like the rest of the outside.

I was new to searching for clues, but this made me think either someone picked up the newspaper on a regular basis, or the newsboy was too scared to drop it off every other day except yesterday.

"Should we ring the doorbell?" Sam looked at me as if I had the answers.

I didn't know and shrugged. "We may as well start there. If someone is home, I'd expect them to answer the door and tell us to scram. If no one answers, we can peek around the back."

Sam took a deep breath and reached one shaky finger out for the doorbell. Deep, horror-movie tones emitted from inside, and we looked at each other with wide eyes.

"Well, that's not promising," I mumbled, catching her nervous nod of agreement from the corner of my eye while we waited for a reaction to the bell.

We must've stood there for at least five minutes, waiting for someone, but heard nothing moving inside the house, and no one came to the door.

"I can't say I'm not relieved," I said, turning to face her.

She wrinkled her nose, glasses shimmying up. "Yeah, me too. But that leaves us back where we started." She pursed her lips, looking to the right then the left before pointing in the direction of the back of the house. "Let's go this way. I see a path going around back. Maybe there's another door we can try."

I followed her as she headed to the right. As expected from the state of the sidewalk in the front, the backyard wasn't any better. I was lucky there wasn't snow yet, or I likely would have managed to slip and impale myself on one of the branches. As it was, I followed with more care than usual behind her to ensure I didn't lose an eye or anything else.

She'd been right about the path, though. It was old and decrepit with broken cobblestones, making the path tricky, but at one point, I could imagine it had probably been nice. The backyard had a wide variety of plants, including a garden that appeared to have been cleaned out for the winter, with several small bushes and other trees I didn't recognize that were still green.

Compared to the rest of what I'd seen, it looked like it had been well-cared for. I filed that tidbit away for later, hoping my slowing brain would allow me to retrieve it in case it proved important.

When I looked to see what Sam was up to, I saw she'd already managed to move aside some of the piled up branches from the back of the house, exposing a set of weathered, wooden doors next to the cement at the base of the house.

"I think it's a cellar door." Excitement lit her eyes, shining from her now filthy face.

"How can you tell?" I moved closer, blinking several times to clear my vision. I hoped it was dirt from the backyard and not the baby cataracts, but I had a feeling my vision was on its way out.

Crapsticks.

I managed to get a good enough look to agree with her. "Oh yeah. It looks like every scary cellar door on old houses in the movies."

She gave me a 'well, duh' look, but her judgement didn't bother me. I was starting to wonder if we were both crazy.

"You aren't the slightest bit worried we seem to be basing all of our clues on things we've seen in awful horror movies? I'm not sure this is the best way to find my mom."

She gave me a patient look. "I know you're saying that because your brain is working slower than usual, but think about everything else that's happened today. I shall list them again." She held up a finger. "One. You're a zombie. Two. Your mom is missing. Three. The creepy new catering place in town is mysteriously empty and we find the food that likely killed you in the dumpster behind it. That's suspect in my books. Four. Finding your mom's cell phone in the dumpster along with your watch suggests you both spent time in the dumpster, or that your stuff was deliberately put there. Which, five. Brings us to this address, the creepiest house in town." She raised her eyebrows and waited.

Grudgingly, I had to agree with her assessment. "Okay, fine. Normally I'd say B grade movies aren't a good place to get either information or a plan of action. However, I will stand corrected by your very logically thought out points. What other B movies can you think of that might apply right now?"

A smile spread over her face. "It's not exactly a horror movie, but you remember that episode of *Supernatural*, where they found all those people in the basement?"

I squinted my eyes, not sure which one she was talking about at first, until I remembered it had also featured a creepy house.

"You mean the one where the witch hunters' mom was in the basement? And they thought they were with her, but it was really a stick person?"

Sam nodded emphatically. "Yeah! That one."

She looked back at the cellar doors and paused. "But now that I'm remembering what happened in the episode, I'm rethinking whether or not to go down there. I'm pretty sure that's how their mom got stabbed in the first place."

I grimaced. That was exactly what had happened. We looked at each other. "Sam and Dean were okay, so maybe we'll be fine if we stick together."

Or more likely we'd end up wicker puppets too. I kept that part in my head as I watched her heave the door open and set it down, wincing when it made a small thump. She looked up with a dark but determined expression. Her voice was barely audible as she stared into the darkness below.

"I sure hope so."

Chapter 7

I was more than a little surprised the door hadn't been locked. I mean, if I were going to be evil and create my own zombie-army, I'd probably lock my secret lair. Maybe that was just me.

We looked at each other, silently debating who would go first.

"Rochambo?" Sam tilted her head, holding her hand out in the familiar rock, paper, scissors position.

I sighed, sounding more like a gust of wind than an actual person. "No. I'll go first. I mean, I am already dead."

I could tell she was relieved by the mere fact she didn't argue with me.

"Thanks. Oh, wait a minute."

It was difficult to tell if there was anything in the cellar from where I was positioned. It loomed below us like a giant mouth and the image of the house eating me flashed through my head. Maybe it would get indigestion from my dead body. It would serve it right.

When Sam turned the flashlight on her phone on, it lit up the stairs enough for me to step inside.

"Thanks. Any night vision I had is completely toast." Sadly, my day vision didn't seem to be far behind.

I slowly picked my way down the handful of rickety wooden stairs, which ended in a dirt floor. I wrinkled my nose. The musty, dead air of the room was a combination of earth and poor ventilation.

I looked up and saw a bare light bulb hanging on a wire. Definitely not up to code. Stacks of shelves made out of old pallets lined the walls and were arranged in rows along the center of the room. If it hadn't been for the fact everything appeared completely derelict and covered in mildew, it kind of resembled a dirty library or the backroom of a store.

I turned to see Sam had pointed her flashlight at something in the far corner. Her eyes flashed as the narrow beam lit up her face, and I caught the movement of her glasses inching up as she slowly stepped toward whatever had caught her attention.

I couldn't see anything but decided to follow anyway, mostly because I could tell something creepy was going on. I didn't want to be that stupid B-movie friend who separated from the herd and died first.

Oh, yeah. I was already dead. Even more reason to stick with her. Maybe I could keep her alive.

Without a word, we headed toward the darkened corner of the room which had captured her attention. Her flashlight fell on a stack of old magazines and what looked like a pile of fabric. I thought it was an odd location for clothing but didn't initially get why she seemed so concerned.

Tilting my head, I squinted harder. My vision was still foggy so I grabbed a stalk of celery out of my hoodie pocket and chowed down. Blinking a few times, I looked at my hand. Better. With my vegetable-improved eyes, I looked back and realized it wasn't a pile of clothing after all.

Swallowing hard, I saw Sam's face glowing an eerie white in the dark. "Alex, isn't that –"

"– Tracy," I nodded, swallowing hard. "Can you check to see if she's still..."

I didn't finish but didn't have to.

As I spoke, she was already bending to take a pulse from Tracy's neck. Thank God for that St. John's Ambulance course she took last summer when she was going through her paramedic phase. She'd since changed her mind of course, but it had been a handy interest while it lasted.

She let out a sigh of relief, and I put my hand against my non-beating heart. When I realized what I'd done, I let it drop. It felt too weird to keep it there when my heart was motionless inside me.

She stood up on an exhale. "Her pulse is good; regular and not too fast. But the fact she didn't wake up when I took it isn't great, unless your mom's friend is a super deep sleeper. She's breathing okay too. I don't see anything obviously wrong, but I don't want to move her in case she has a spinal cord injury or something."

"What should we do? I mean, if Tracy's here and unconscious, maybe my mom is around too."

Sam looked uncertain. "I think we need to call it in. Tracy needs to go to the hospital."

I nodded, trying to think. I nibbled on my fingernail, spitting it out in disgust when the whole thing came off in one piece.

"Yeah, I know. But what if that makes whoever did this take off, or worse, hurt my mom? Tracy looks...well, at least she has a pulse." I looked down and grimaced. "I wouldn't say she looks too lively. Can you text 911? I don't want to get held up with questions until we see if my mom is in the house or not."

Sam shook her head. "Nope, it won't let you do that. But I can dial 911 and hide my phone somewhere."

I nodded, considering the possibilities. "That would buy us a little time. We might be able to get through the rest of the house before they show up. And if we don't give them an address, they'll probably have a hard time finding us but at least somebody would be nearby looking, which I like. Especially if things hit the fan. Okay, let's do it. But after we check the rest of the cellar."

We canvassed the rest of the basement, more than happy not to find any other surprise bodies or anything else. Nothing stood out as particularly unusual. Just stacks and stacks of pots, pans, and canned goods. It kind of looked like a bomb shelter prep unit.

I glanced at the canned food, noting most seemed to contain vegetables or other perishable food items. Nothing looked weird or human, which I was grateful about. I'd begun to worry I'd find pickled toes or something similar.

My hunger stirred at the thought of pickles and I rummaged in my pocket, discovering I was almost out of vegetables. Pursing my lips, I considered whether or not it was safe to eat creepy vegetables in a stranger's basement after you'd broken in.

Well, since I was already dead and they didn't know I was coming, it probably wouldn't matter. Even if they were full of botulism, they couldn't kill me.

I liberated a few small jars of beets off the shelf. Anything pickled should hopefully be safe. The only problem was they didn't exactly fit into the hoodie I was wearing.

Dammit, should've brought a backpack.

Or worn pants.

Putting one back, I compromised and carried one jar in each hand.

While I'd been getting stocked up, Sam had dialed her phone and hidden it in one of the pots on a back shelf. I took a step then reconsidered and popped the lid off one of the jars. As I dumped the beets into my mouth, fireworks went off in my head.

Prior to the vegetables hitting my tongue, I hadn't been super hungry. But it was like a switch had been flipped. Suddenly, I couldn't focus on anything else. Finishing one, I opened the other jar and downed it too.

I rolled my eyes at the exquisite flavor, regretting the movement immediately at the feel of them grinding against their sockets. When I reopened them, both jars were empty, but I was still ravenous. I stumbled back to the shelf and systematically opened another three jars without bothering to see what was inside. A medley of pickled beets, cucumbers, and radishes delighted my taste buds, and I wolfed them down with greedy joy.

Sam came around the corner and stopped abruptly, staring at me as I polished off jar number six. "Um, Alex..." She gestured to her face. "You look like you just ate someone with purple blood. You're totally stained. Can you at least try to eat like a person?"

I shrugged, feeling my hunger abate as I swallowed one last mouthful. "Sorry, I wasn't planning on it. I was unexpectedly famished. But, hey, bonus, I can see again."

I smiled and gave her jazz hands, impressed by how much smoother the movement was now. She didn't comment at first, but when she saw how many jars were empty, her jaw dropped.

"Wow. That might actually be a world record for pickled beets in one standing. Maybe you should bring a couple jars with, just in case."

"Yeah, I was planning on it, but remembered I didn't have a bag and then, well, I got carried away." I grinned sheepishly, wondering if my lips were as purple as my fingers were becoming. Probably.

Giving me a look of studied patience, she gestured to the wall beside me to something white. For the first time, I noticed the huge stack of plastic bags.

"Oh. Ha, ha, ha. Yeah, that should work."

She shook her head. "All right, I'm doing all the thinking from now on. I'd double bag it to be on the safe side, if I were you."

I stuffed six jars of beets into the double-bagged plastic as she'd suggested then followed her to the closed door at the top of the stairs.

Chapter 8

Just like in every B grade horror movie I'd ever seen, the stairs were bare gray boards, almost rotted out in places. They creaked menacingly with every step, and I bit back the urge to groan. That was far too close to completing the horror theme for my liking. I could see from Sam's expression she was having a similar issue.

As she was prone to fits of nervous giggles, I was glad she was maintaining her cool so far.

When we reached the door at the top, it loomed in front of us with its plain dark wood and old brass rusted doorknob. Sam hesitated, looking at me as she gnawed the inside of her lip.

"Go on, open it," I said, pushing her forward. Absently, I noticed the skin on the back of my left hand starting to peel.

She put her hand on the doorknob and pushed, causing it to shriek with an ungodly, deafening sound in the silence. She stopped the moment it was wide enough for us to squeeze through, waiting to make a move until she was sure no one had heard the eerie creaking. Although loud to us, I hoped it wasn't the fire alarm it had felt like in my head.

Cautiously, we squeezed through into the darkened hallway without pushing the door open any further. It had been midday when we'd entered, but you would never have guessed from the dim light filtering in through to the windowless hallway from the rooms.

Sam looked at me. Once she had my attention, she pointed to the left then the right. I shrugged and pointed to the right. For some reason, right seemed luckier than going left. But maybe that was another old superstition as well.

At the end of the hall, it branched into a T. This time, the path was brighter heading left. We nodded at each other and began walking toward the light. Tiptoeing as quietly as we could, Sam went first, peering around every corner before proceeding.

When she got to the end of the hall and peeked into the room the light was coming from, she drew back immediately, her eyes wide and confused. Frowning, I lifted my hands in the universal 'what gives' gesture, but she just shook her head and moved out of the way.

I shuffled forward to see for myself, handing her the bag of beets to hold. We were still trying not to talk, but I caught her nose wrinkle as I passed by. A vague sense of sadness swamped me. It hadn't just been my imagination.

I was definitely starting to smell.

A surge of bravery coursed through me. What did I have left to lose? I was now vegetable-fueled and decomposing fast. I probably didn't even have a full twenty-four hours left, so it wasn't like I could be killed. I wasn't even sure I could be tortured the way they did in horror movies, because it was possible I wouldn't feel it. Even if I did, it would be short-lived.

Thinking about Sam, my mom, and her friend, Tracy, I kept my bravery in check. I had to find out what was going on before I did anything either brave or stupid. My eyes blinked as they adjusted to the light in the room. In front of me was a woman I'd never seen before. She looked surprisingly...normal.

But what she was doing was anything but.

My mouth dropped open so rapidly I had to put my hand up to catch my lower jaw. It wobbled as I slowly, carefully, pushed it back into place. If my heart hadn't already stopped, the scene in front of me might have done it for me.

In a cozy kitchen, which would have been suitable for tea and crumpets, was an assembly line. Jars filled with unrecognizable items lined one wall of shelves and on the floor beneath it were three people, tied up and gagged.

My mom was in the middle of the hostages, glaring.

The cheerful woman was standing at the stove, stirring a pot as she hummed to herself. When one of the people on the floor whimpered behind their gag, she turned to them with a twinkle and put one fist on her hip as she shook her wooden spoon at them.

"Oh, hush there. You've absolutely nothing to worry about, my dear. As soon as I'm done making this potion, your troubles will be over. I'll need you all to taste-test it though, to make sure it works."

She turned her back to the prisoners to stir the pot once more. I watched as her eyebrows knitted together and she bit her lower lip with even, white teeth. If she was a witch, she looked a lot more like Glinda than the Wicked Witch of the West. Or Mrs. Claus. Maybe that was why she'd been able to tie up so many people on her own.

If she was alone.

A thought struck me—how had Tracy had ended up dumped in the basement? Had she already tried a potion on her and it hadn't worked? I looked at Sam, but I couldn't ask her anything without being overheard. Regardless, I didn't want my mom taste-testing whatever was in that pot if it was anything like the lasagna.

I looked around for something, anything, to use as a weapon. I was hoping the woman's power lay in her ability to make food or potions, because if she could throw something at me like a lightning bolt, I was pretty much screwed. I didn't see anything in the kitchen so I pulled back to hide behind the wall again.

Sam's eyebrows were raised and I nodded grimly. Squinting, I looked at the dark hallway, seeing nothing except the bag of canned beets I'd brought up from the basement. Maybe I could use them. But first, I needed to power up.

While Sam looked on in disgust, I opened the first jar and downed it. The same overwhelming hunger lunged at me, and I systematically opened the next two jars and swallowed them whole as well. As I slowly regained control, my vision improved and the numbness which had been creeping over my feet receded.

I carefully considered the remaining jars. If I ate them, they'd give me more energy, but the bag might be too light for how I was planning to use it. I carefully compared the weights of an empty jar with a full jar and shook my head, placing only the three full jars in the double bag before spinning the bag shut. It would be easier to swing a smaller, heavier bag.

I turned back to watch the woman put the ladle down and clap with joy as she turned to her captive audience. "It's perfect. Now, who would like to be the first volunteer?"

When no one made a sound, some of her excitement faded and she folded her arms in front of her. "What? No one wants to see if they can live forever? Well, that *is* a disappointment. Never mind, I'll do the honors."

The moment took a surreal dip into childishness as she began to do eenie, meenie, meenie, moe. Deciding her distraction might be my only opening, I rushed forward while she faced her captives and swung the bag as hard as I could, slugging her over the back of the head with a three-jar beet bomb.

Chapter 9

Betty Crocker dropped like my mom's chiffon cake.

I looked into the stunned faces of the three people tied up on the floor, knowing my own eyes were as wide as they would go as I moved my gaze down to the woman I'd knocked out.

Blood trickled from where the bag had made contact on the side of her head, and I knelt down gingerly to check her pulse.

My index finger was black. Crap.

I quickly hid my hand, pretty sure I wouldn't be able to feel anything with it and not wanting my mom to notice.

"Um, Sam? Can you come here please? I need some help."

She entered the room and halted at the sight of the woman on the ground, her face lighting up when she realized she was unconscious. "Oh my God, wicked! Who knew beets could do so much damage on the outside as well?"

She chortled at her joke as I gestured impatiently for her to come closer.

"I need you to check her to see if she's still alive. My fingers aren't exactly... sensitive at the moment." I opened my eyes wide, glaring meaningfully at her.

When she nodded without delay, I knew she understood.

"Of course, no problem!" Smoothly, she assessed the pulse from the woman's neck and stood up. "It's still there. We should move fast. I have a feeling she's going to wake up unhappy."

I flicked my gaze down at the sticky blood and winced. "Can you untie my mom first? I'll take the gags off the other two while you do that."

We set to work and the instant that my mom's gag was out, a string of expletives I'd never heard her use emerged for a solid thirty seconds.

Sam and I stepped back involuntarily.

At that moment, I was more afraid of my mom than the woman who'd tied her up.

"You know, I think even after everything else that's happened to us today, your mom's mouth is possibly the most shocking thing of all."

Sam looked at her with a wariness I'd never seen before and I nodded. It was a little hard to take in on top of everything else.

"Wow, Mom. And you've threatened to wash my mouth out with soap? For shame."

I hoped a joke would lighten the mood, but it didn't. She glared as she turned her fury to the unconscious woman, practically spitting flames in her direction.

"You'd be swearing too if you'd been tied up by this psycho-granny."

"Yeah, probably. We've already dialed 911. Someone should be here soon. What happened? How did you get here and who are these two?" I pointed at the other hostages Sam was currently releasing.

She shrugged. "No idea. I came here last night, after you started acting funny from the lasagna." She gave me a suspicious look, then squinted as she gave me a thorough once over. "You're wearing an awful lot of eye make-up. And is that how you always dress when I'm not around?"

I shook my head, nervously flicking my eyes to Sam. "No, Mom; it's Halloween. I put some of my costume on early."

She clearly didn't believe me but thankfully, chose not to pursue it.

"Anyway, I went back to the caterer to find out if she'd sold me a bad batch and that was what had made you sick. I'd been making arrangements for a Halloween party at Tracy's tonight." She paused, her eyebrows knitting together as she looked around. "Where is she? I was going to surprise her with a small party, but after you ate the lasagna and started to look kind of green, I texted her and let her know I was going to have a talk with the caterer. I was planning to cancel our order, but when I got to the shop, the front was empty."

Sam listened in as she untied the others. "Did you see the lasagna in the garbage out back?"

My mom nodded. "Yes. And I saw *her* as well."

I followed her gaze to the still body of the angelic appearing caterer from hell.

"I don't understand. How did you get from the store to here? We found your phone in the dumpster, which I thought was a little strange, even under the circumstances."

She looked embarrassed. If I wasn't mistaken, she may have even been blushing.

"Yeah, that's my fault. I didn't want her to see me, so I hid when I saw her coming to dump the rest of the lasagna. That was when I texted Tracy to let her know what was going on."

"And you dropped your phone in the dumpster?" Sam piped up, unabashedly curious.

I didn't blame her, because so was I.

My mom grimaced. "Yeah."

I shook my head, brain sluggishly trying to connect the dots. "Wait a minute, if you were in the dumpster, or near the dumpster and dropped your phone, how did you know the address?"

My mom waived my question away. "That's easy. I found out where the caterer lived when I was placing the order earlier in the week. I was surprised but didn't think much of it at the time. I mean, the house has got great bones. I thought maybe she had a fetish for flipping."

When both Sam and I gave her incredulous looks, she stopped to roll her eyes. Someday I hoped to master the eye roll the way she had. It was truly impressive.

"Okay, cut the crap. Everyone in town knows this house is haunted."

Sam's derisive reply was close to my thoughts, but when my mom narrowed her eyes, I pressed my lips together and kept my opinion to myself.

"Anyway, once you got sick I figured something strange was up, and I needed to know what. Apparently, while I was doing my best to be sneaky, I lost my phone in the process. I didn't want to waste time garbage picking, so I decided to drive over."

When both Sam and I glared, my mom held her hands up in self-defense.

"I know, that's exactly what happens in those stupid movies you guys watch. Normally, I'd say you're totally overreacting. I'll never mock you for watching those things again after this happened." She stopped to look at the woman on the floor. "How did you find me anyway?"

Sam looked at me, but I wasn't sure what to say either so I deflected.

"I woke up this morning feeling strange. Odd, but better than I did last night. In fact, I'm not really sure what happened after the lasagna. I woke up this morning with leaves in my hair and dirty hands." I grimaced, adding ruefully, "it's possible I spent the night in a dumpster too. Anyway, at first I thought both you and dad were missing until I remembered he was away. Once I realized it was just you who'd been home with me, I wondered if you would've gone back to the place you bought the lasagna to give them a piece of your mind."

She started laughing. "I'm getting predictable in my old age, aren't I?" When we both nodded, she chuckled again. "Yes, basically that's what happened. I thought you were sick, so I went back to the caterer's to give the person I talked with a piece of my mind. After I followed her back to the house, well, that's when things get fuzzy for me."

I wondered if she'd been knocked out when she reached up to check her head.

"How did you end up hogtied in the kitchen?" Sam gestured to her hands and feet.

My mom raised her eyebrows. "No idea. The last thing I remember was ringing the doorbell last night around eight or nine. Next thing I know, I'm waking up tied up beside a stove. Hey, did you happen to see Tracy on the way in?"

I nodded slowly. "Yeah, we found her in the basement when we snuck in. She was unconscious, but we aren't sure what happened to her. That's why we dialed 911."

My mom looked worried. "I should go check on her."

She started to stand, but Sam put a hand out to stop her.

"Maybe we should stick together right now, Mrs. N. I don't know if there's anyone else in the house but until the police or the paramedics get here, we're safer in a group."

I was impressed by how wise Sam sounded, right up until she nodded her head and assumed a paranoid expression, looking both ways.

"This is what I know from years of the very best of the worst, bad horror movies out there. Stay together and never go off looking for anyone."

My mom sighed. I knew she agreed with Sam's logic, even if the source was slightly suspect, but was worried about her friend. By now, the other two hostages were standing. While nervous, they appeared relieved to be out of their ropes.

I gave them what I tried to make a reassuring smile, but when my lip stuck to one of my teeth, it turned into an Elvis curl instead. "Hi, my name is Alex. This is my friend Sam, and well, I see you've already met my mom."

The man held out his hand. "Hi, my name is Ken Anderson and this is my wife Sandy. I don't know what happened. The last thing I remember, we were out for an evening walk in the neighborhood."

"I thought I heard a cat crying," Sandy interjected. "It sounded like it was hurt. I convinced Ken we should trespass in the backyard. That's the last thing I remember."

"She probably got you then," Sam said, matter-of-factly. "We found Tracy in the cellar. I'm wondering if she tested one of her potions on Tracy already, or if she was just keeping her downstairs in case she needed another victim to trial something on later."

My mom looked like she was about to charge off looking for Tracy, so I tried to distract her. "How about we all make our way toward the front yard and wait for the ambulance?"

Ken and Sandy smiled and moved into the hallway behind Sam. Clearly, they thought my idea was brilliant. My mom looked a little more doubtful, but I was sure it was because she was concerned for her friend, not because she hoped to stay here any longer than she had to.

"Okay, let's go. But I want to go check on Tracy once..."

"Help arrives." Sam finished my mom's sentence.

My mom smiled. "Exactly right. Sam, thanks for being you. I never thought I'd be so happy to see you here, but I'm glad to know my daughter can count on you to watch her back and keep her from accidentally dying on one of her adventures."

Sam's eyes widened slightly, and she turned abruptly, gesturing to the door with a maniacal cheer. "Absolutely! Okay, everyone. Let's jet!"

She winced when she caught sight of the old woman still crumpled on the floor. The patch of blood was slightly larger now. "What should we do with her?"

I felt guilty. I'd done that, even though she'd deserved it. She'd tied up my mom and may have done something permanent to Tracy, not to mention my entire zombification bit. But I'd never hurt anyone before. It made me feel sick to my stomach to see blood because of something I'd done, and not just because I was off animal products.

"I'm not sure. I mean, it would make sense to leave her here and just let the cops deal with it."

But even as I looked down at her, I knew I needed answers. That same odd sense of bravery, which had filled me when I realized I literally had nothing left to lose, made me want to stay and ask the villain of my story a few questions.

Mainly, why the hell was I a teenage vegetarian zombie?

"You know, Sam, on second thought, I'll be right there."

Both Sam and my mom looked at me with varying degrees of surprise. Sam nodded almost immediately, giving me a sad smile.

"Sure. You still have your cell on you, right?"

I nodded, taking it out of my pocket and holding it up.

"Okay, text...darn it!" Sam stopped and I remembered she'd tucked her phone into a pot in the basement.

"You can text me." I remembered I still had my mom's phone and fished it out for them. "Or I'll text my mom. Don't worry, I'll be okay for a few minutes. Not to mention if you guys wait outside, you'll be able to see the lights and sirens in the next couple minutes. You can direct them in when they get here. I want to make sure she's still breathing."

Sam knew 'breathing' was code for 'I'm going to attempt to interrogate this person' and winked. "Okay, see you soon."

"I thought you said we're supposed to stick together? Rule number one of horror movies. You literally just said that to me."

My mom stood with her arms crossed, clearly not willing to go along with my decision without a better reason. Then again, my mom didn't realize I was already dead, something I wasn't about to fill her in on if I didn't have to.

"Yeah, Mom, but remember, it's okay when the heroine does it."

I put my hand over my heart, still weirded out not to feel anything when I did that, and batted my eyelashes at her while praying none would fall off.

"And clearly, I'm the heroine in this story. I mean, I just rescued three people who were tied up in a kitchen. Besides, it's a straight walk from the kitchen to the front door. You can leave it open and still see me from there."

Arms still crossed, she narrowed her eyes even further. By this point, they were hardly open. Normally I would have been quaking in my shoes as it was her 'you're grounded' face, but I had bigger worries.

"The only reason I'm even buying your shoddy logic is because I know something strange is happening and you seem to have a plan. So instead of getting in the way of what you're doing, I'll let you do what you think is best if you promise to explain everything when this is over."

Using the hand that was currently resting on my heart, I crossed it and looked earnestly into her eyes. "Absolutely, Mom. I promise."

With that, everyone followed Sam out. My mom trailed behind, throwing one last troubled look over her shoulder before she went. I tried to smile reassuringly, but my lip stuck again. I rubbed my nose, surreptitiously pushing it down. She sighed before turning away.

I realized for the first time how lucky I was to have a mom who trusted me. It was too bad I wouldn't be around much longer. She'd joked more than once the reason they'd had a kid in the first place was to look after them in their old age. While I knew it wasn't the only reason, I could only imagine how hard it would be on her to find out I had died before her and had an unnatural taste for veggies.

Man, being a zombie was such a bummer.

Chapter 10

Brushing away all thoughts of mortality, I turned to the woman on the ground. She'd started to stir as the others exited. I wasn't sure whether or not I was happy she was waking up but it did align with my goals to interrogate her, which was convenient.

She groaned again, bearing a remarkable resemblance to what Betty Crocker with a hangover would look like, but when she opened her eyes and saw me standing above her, she didn't react the way I expected her to. Instead of being angry or even surprised, her head tilted back and she gave me a knowing look.

"I wondered if I'd see you today." She struggled to sit upright, keeping her eyes fixed on my face as she moved.

"What's that supposed to mean? I mean, why would you expect to see me? You don't even know who I am."

She tilted her head in acknowledgment as she gave me a small smile. "You're right. We've never met. But I do, in fact, know you. As you may have already suspected, I'm the reason you've woken up the way you did today."

A surge of satisfaction flooded through me.

"Aha! I knew it! Wait, what do you mean?"

While I was happy to have her admission of guilt, her reply didn't tell me squat. I needed more details and preferably, a cure.

She made no attempt to stand. Pulling her knees up to her chest as she rested against the wall, she leaned her head back and winced when it made contact with the lump I'd given her.

"Ouch." She brought one hand up to rub the area, grimacing when she took her hand away and saw blood on her fingers. "What did you hit me with, anyway?"

I pointed to the bag of beets on the floor, which strangely enough didn't look any worse for the wear. Apparently those old mason jars were tough. They knocked her out and none of the jars even looked cracked.

Huh, maybe I hadn't needed to double bag after all.

The woman chuckled, an oddly infectious laugh that didn't match her angelic look. "Et tu, Bruté?" She shook her head, giving the beets a chiding look.

The beets sat in their plastic bag, not caring.

She narrowed her eyes as she regarded me again. "If you must know, I was experimenting in the kitchen when your mother happened by. She wouldn't take no for an answer about the lasagna you ate last night." She sighed, pressing her lips together. "I'd already determined the batch was bad and was in the process of deciding if I should throw them away when she arrived. Let's just say your mom is a forceful woman and wouldn't take no for an answer. Before I could get a word in edgewise, she'd thrown a twenty on the counter and left with a container."

"You're kidding."

Then again, this was my mom she was talking about. I could see her doing that if it smelled as good as I remembered.

At my look of disbelief, she shrugged. "Hey, I tried to stop her. It was like trying to argue with a pigeon- completely pointless. I'd hoped I was wrong about the batch, but obviously I was not."

I shook my head, tightening my lips when another strand of hair fell off my head in front of me. "All right, so maybe you didn't mean to do this to me. Why the hell did you have everybody tied up in the kitchen then? That's not exactly something someone does while trying to fix a mistake."

I crossed my arms and began tapping my foot. By now, she'd started to slowly inch her way up the wall into a standing position. She was swaying a little, but I tensed what was left of my slowly gelling muscles in anticipation of attack just in case.

"I never said I was great at being good, my dear. However, people suddenly dropping dead in a zombiefied state is not good for anyone's business. I've been in this house for a while now and I like to keep a low profile."

When she stopped, I could see she was deciding how much to say. Now I was curious. "Low profile? How does kidnapping people count as low profile? I thought my mom said you had just moved in?"

I wasn't sure I actually wanted the details, but a vague notion had occurred to me that if I kept her talking long enough, back-up would arrive to save us all.

She sniffed. "The catering gig is new, that's true. It's something a little different I'm trying out. Dabbling in potions on the black market with people who know what they're looking for can be fun, but it's not exactly easy to submit those receipts to the tax man. Dead bodies showing up on my doorstep is even harder to explain and certainly not part of my usual business model."

My lack of comprehension at her explanation was apparent and she waved her hand dismissively.

"Anyway, that isn't important. What is important is you not falling to pieces. I may be able to cover up everything else that happened today, but it's much harder to hide teenagers when they start dying from suspicious causes. Not good for business at all. If you must know, when you and your friend so valiantly broke in here, I was testing an antidote on my guests."

"Guests? Wait—an antidote?"

A nagging sense of unease grew in my sluggish midsection even as the words left my mouth.

Betty Crocker shrugged. "For the lasagna, of course."

My head dropped as I looked at her through my sparse eyelashes. "Do you mean to tell me you made them eat the lasagna?"

Betty Crocker laughed, and it sounded like church bells ringing. "I didn't force anyone to eat anything. In fact, I had a dinner party in the wee hours of last night with your mother and the Andersons. They ate it, willingly, and even asked for seconds."

I shook my head as I tried to piece together what she was saying. "So why were they tied up? And why is my mom's friend in the basement?"

She blinked. "There's someone in my basement?"

I groaned and Betty Crocker covered her mouth, muffling a giggle. When I glared at her, she did her best to look neutral, but it was too late. Secretly, I agreed with her. Groans were damn funny in my current state.

"I didn't realize there was someone in my basement, they must've gotten turned around, or something." She squinted her eyes, looking just past my ear. "It's no problem though. I am assuming you've already called 911?"

She appeared more exasperated than angry, and when I nodded, she sighed.

"Oh, bother. Well, I'm sure you don't trust me, but while your mom may have a pulse at the moment, it's not going to last much longer. I suggest if you and your mom would like to see tomorrow it may be wise to bring everyone inside to the dining room table." She pointed impatiently at the large black pot on the stove. "If you'll allow me to give everyone this potion, you can be on your way with no one the wiser."

I pursed my lips, thinking about the options before me. "How much time do we have before we need to decide? My mom and the Andersons look totally normal. How can I believe what you're telling me is true? How do I know this isn't an elaborate ploy to make more zombie puppets?"

She watched me calmly. "You don't know, of course. And you're not wrong in thinking I might be totally evil. But I promise you, I'm not stupid."

She walked cautiously back to the stove without taking her eyes off of me.

"This town is my home as much as it is yours. I may not be what you would consider an upstanding member of the community, but I have a place here, every bit as much as you do, and have no interest in moving. This house has been in my family for a hundred years. I plan to make sure it's in my family for another hundred more. Which means I need to clear this situation up immediately."

I considered her words, then pointed out the biggest flaw. "How do we know the potion won't kill us so that you can just hide our bodies instead?"

She rolled her eyes. "Murder is so ordinary. And not nearly as efficient at getting rid of someone as you might think. There are always clues. Someone will generally trace things back, no matter how careful one is. I'd rather not have to deal with humans and their stupid laws and morality. I prefer my quiet life the way it is. If you don't believe me, feel free to test the potion yourself. After all," she paused, gesturing to my head and down my body. "You're already out of time. If my estimation is correct, you have less than six hours before you stop moving around entirely."

I exhaled. She was right. I'd been thinking the same thing. While the vegetables were keeping me powered for now, they weren't aiding me in regenerating any longer and barely helping me to maintain. At the rate I was decomposing, I wouldn't make it to Zach's party. Even if I did, the shape I'd be arriving in wouldn't be remotely kissable.

"Fine," I snapped, moving to stand beside her at the stove. "How quickly will it work? Because the authorities are probably less than five minutes away."

Betty Crocker raised her hands. "I'm not sure. I've never tried it. My guess is before then. In fact, if I've done it correctly, you should know pretty much immediately."

I bit my lip, shuddering at the disgusting flavor of rotting meat. I literally had nothing to lose. "All right, I'll try it."

"Perfect."

She smiled, but the evil I half-expected to see in it wasn't there. She wore the same curiosity and satisfaction of a parent who'd gotten you to agree to finish your medicine and was now interested to see if it worked.

She carefully scooped out a small amount, placing it in a wide-based cup and blew on it until the steam stopped rising, then handed it over. She watched with anticipation as I looked at the glass and I raised it to her.

"Bottoms up!"

I'd expected it to taste disgusting, like most medicine, but it was every bit as delicious as the lasagna had been. Maybe even more so. It tasted like apple cider spiced with just the right amount of cinnamon, like a fall harvest, and everything warm and lovely that came with cooler weather.

I drank the entire glass, thinking that if it was poison, at least it tasted good going down.

As I placed the glass on the counter, a burning sensation pierced my stomach. Pain spread out from there, sending shocks of electricity and bolts of pain everywhere. Every molecule in my body felt as if it had caught fire in a lava-filled lake.

I screamed and fell to the floor, writhing in agony as my body exploded into a hot, white light of pain. I had no idea how long it continued. It could have been minutes or hours.

As the pain slowly began to recede, I opened my eyes and saw my mom sitting beside me with a face full of worry.

"Mom? You're supposed to be outside, waiting for the ambulance."

I was oddly irritated by her presence, even though I could tell she was distraught. She brushed away a tear from her face and forced a smile.

"I heard you scream and came to see what was happening. I found you on the floor, and *her* standing over there by the stove. You started to stir before I could do anything."

My mom glared at Betty Crocker, who was standing beside the stove completely unperturbed. When I added my glare to my mom's, she merely raised an eyebrow.

"I said it would work quickly; I never said it wouldn't hurt."

"Fair enough."

I got up slowly and reassessed my physical state. The first thing I noticed when I looked at my hands was the color was no longer the weird off-white gray they'd been a moment earlier. I ran my fingers through my hair, pulling my hand away and smiled when I didn't pull out a chunk of hair as well. Almost scared to verify it, I placed my fingertips on my wrist to search for the most important part.

A pulse.

It was there, bounding steadily along at a more rapid clip than usual.

I looked at Betty Crocker with amazement. "It worked!"

"Of course it worked, silly girl. You think I'm a noob? The only reason the lasagna didn't work out was because the oregano was old." She huffed, crossing her arms.

I realized I'd managed to insult her, which wasn't what I'd intended. At least, not this time. "I'm sorry for doubting you. But, reasons."

She nodded. "Of course. You would've been stupid not to. Now, can you get the others? I'm assuming you believe me now?"

I nodded, standing with my mom's help and bit my cheek. I was overjoyed not to remove skin and have that God-awful taste in my mouth.

"I'll let them know, but it may be a hard sell. And Tracy's still in the basement." I looked at the front door, feeling nervous. "We might actually need the paramedics even if you didn't do anything. She was unconscious when we found her."

The woman nodded thoughtfully, and to my surprise, agreed. "It may still work. If you can get the Andersons and your mother to sit down in the dining room, I'll bring everyone a mug of cider. When the paramedics get here, you may direct them to the basement. As I didn't do anything and you didn't do anything, my deduction is that she must have fallen in the basement while snooping around. Much easier to explain than a dead body would be." She raised her eyebrows.

I nodded. "Sure, I'll let them know."

I headed to the door with my mom trailing after me.

"Why are you speaking with her like that? She had me and two other people tied up! The woman is a nut job and needs to be arrested."

She was confused and irate but I wasn't sure how much of my explanation she'd believe, so I stuck to trying to calm her down.

"I promise I'll explain everything when we get home. I don't think you're going to believe me right now and we don't have time to get into it. Trust me when I say you and the Andersons need to drink the cider crazy Betty Crocker is going to give you. I've already drank it and I'm fine. It's delicious, but has a bit of a kick at the end."

To put it mildly.

My mom tightened her jaw and glared at me for a moment. Thankfully, she didn't argue. "You better believe we're going to have a chat when we get home."

We walked to the front step and found Sam huddled with the Andersons. The second she saw me, she sprang up and clutched me tightly.

"Alex! Oh my God! You're..." She trailed off, looking at my face. Happiness sparkled in her eyes.

"Yeah, it's wonderful. Turns out, evil Betty Crocker had an antidote after all. Now, we need to get everybody to the dining room so that they can take it as well."

Her eyebrows almost shot up to her hairline. "You mean when we walked in on her about to give them the stuff in the pot..."

I nodded. "Yup. That was the antidote."

"Which means..."

"... They've all had lasagna."

Sam immediately turned to my mother and the Andersons. "All right everyone, back in the house. There's one more thing you need to do before we leave. Alex already tested it, so you'll be totally fine. However, we have reason to believe if you don't drink something before you go, things with your health will go downhill fast." Sam's grimace was not reassuring.

The Andersons were clearly confused by the sudden about-face and moved closer to each other. Sandy Anderson bit her lip and looked at her husband.

"I don't know, honey. What do you think? It's crazy to go back inside a house we were just tied up in, isn't it? It is, right?"

He drew his eyebrows together, assessing us for a long moment before he raised his hands and let them fall to his sides.

"It is, but maybe we should see what they have to say. After all, they were the ones who untied us. I doubt they'd lead us back inside if it wasn't safe." He looked at us again, giving both of us a stern dad-look. "You'd better know what you're talking about."

I smiled, hoping my hesitancy didn't overpower my attempt at certainty. It wasn't like I could explain any of this in a way that was believable. If I tried, they definitely wouldn't accept the drink.

"Trust me."

I tried to infuse my voice with as much authority and wisdom as I could. But as I was about five-foot-two and recently dead/newly alive, I wasn't sure I'd sold anyone on the plan. Regardless of their doubts though, by some miracle, everyone followed me inside to the dining room.

Sam brought up the rear, nervously glancing at the open front door behind us. I knew she was looking for any sign of emergency lights. So far, nothing.

It was a darn good thing nobody was actually dying.

The Andersons sat across from my mom at an oak dining room table large enough for at least ten people. With only the three of them there, the table looked oddly barren and even larger. Sam sat down to the right of Mrs. Anderson, and I sat beside my mom.

Within seconds of everyone sitting in their places, three mugs of cider entered the room on a tray carried by the deceptively kindly-appearing, possibly evil, Betty Crocker doppelgänger. The smell wafting from them was appealing and I relaxed. Surely, if it smelled good they'd at least take a sip.

I waited while they looked at the mugs in front of them with a mixture of apprehension, distrust, and the expression a five-year-old gets when being encouraged to try brussel sprouts for the first time.

Just then, the faint sound of sirens in the distance became audible.

Time was running out.

I turned to my mom with wide, pleading eyes as sweat began to trickle down my back. "Mom, trust me. You need to drink that right now. It'll be really bad if you don't."

The sirens sounded like they were right outside the house.

To my surprise, my mother took the mug off the table and chugged it. When she was done, she wiped her mouth with the back of her right hand and crossed her arms. "Now what?"

I blinked, half expecting her to scream and fall down the way I had. When nothing happened, the Andersons shrugged and picked up their mugs, clinking them together then downed theirs as well.

Nothing there, either.

A wave of relief washed over me. Apparently, excruciating pain and hot tingles only happened if you actually had to be brought back to life.

A knock on the door echoed in the house, causing us all to turn.

"Hello? We received a call from around this address, but we're not sure this is the right house. Dispatch wasn't able to get any information from the cell the call was placed with. Your door was open, so we thought we'd check and see if anyone here knows anything."

Betty Crocker laughed, a tinkling sound like bells and wiped her hands off on her cheery, floral apron. "Oh, heavens to Betsy! Yes, this is the right house. One of the girls lost her phone downstairs shortly after she called for help. We had just sat down for a nice visit with some harvest apple cider when we heard a noise downstairs. When we checked it out, we found an unconscious woman in the basement. We called to make sure she got the help she needs but must have gotten flustered."

I watched as she batted her eyelashes and smiled at the officer. She looked so friendly and innocent and even though her version didn't make sense, I totally bought it. I wondered if she'd thrown up a glamour. Was that what it was called?

Whatever she'd done, the police officer relaxed and smiled at her.

"Let's check it out, shall we?" He paused, turning to speak into the radio in a voice too low to make out everything he was saying. When he was done, he smiled again. "Show me where you found her. I called a bus to this address."

I looked at Sam, mouthing, "bus?"

Sam mouthed back a reply. "Ambulance."

Ah. Of course

. Stepping forward, I looked up at the officer and gestured him to follow me into the hall. "I can show you where we found her."

He acknowledged the rest of the group with a small incline of his head. "Be right back. If the paramedics show up, send them on down."

I was nervous what we'd find when went into the basement, but Tracy was exactly where we'd left her. She was unconscious but appeared otherwise uninjured. While I couldn't be certain evil Betty Crocker hadn't given her something, I was slightly more confident whatever she'd done wouldn't harm her in the long run.

She had saved my life, after all, and after the antidote, I believed her logic about bodies being hard to hide if nothing else.

I stood back while the police officer knelt down and checked her pulse the way Sam had. I held my breath as he spoke into his radio again, and this time I could hear some of what he was saying.

"Mid-forties... Caucasian... Average height and weight..."

I tried not to make noise as he gave information to who I assumed were the paramedics. I shuffled my feet as nerves overwhelmed me. Would he think I'd done this to her? To my untrained eye, the room was immaculate and I couldn't see any helpful clues. I had no idea how the witch was going to spin this. The corner where Tracy had been found wasn't anywhere close to the window. I hoped it would be her problem to explain, not mine.

Boots on the stairs followed us almost immediately as the paramedics arrived, took one look at Tracy, and loaded her onto a narrow stretcher. I was impressed by how smoothly they navigated the rickety wooden stairs, now silent and sturdy, under their calm and determined movements.

I brought up the caboose as I followed the police officer back to the dining room where the others were waiting with matching expressions of concern on their faces. Everyone except for my mom, who was looking between the officer and Betty Crocker with barely suppressed rage.

The same look she'd given me the extremely rare times I'd returned after curfew.

If there weren't other people present, I was positive my mom would've given her a large chunk of her mind. As I'd almost lost mine due to supernatural decay from a lousy lasagna,

I knew it was time to get her out of there before she could open her mouth and say something to cause Betty to change her mind and go ape-shit on us for real.

"I'm sorry Officer... Jameson." I squinted to read his name tag, smiling as bright as I could when he looked at me.

"Yes?"

"Can we leave? My friend and I have a Halloween party to get ready for, and it's getting late." I looked at my filthy watch, grimacing dramatically. "The party starts soon and we still need to prepare our costumes."

Sam jumped in with her two cents. "Please, sir. If you let us go, I'll give you my cell number and you can call me anytime."

Just when I thought, *hoped*, she was done, she blurted out the one thing I didn't want anyone else to know.

"Alex has a crush on the guy throwing the party. She's hoping he'll ask her out tonight."

My mouth dropped open in horror and my cheeks burned with embarrassment. "Sam! That was supposed to be our secret!"

Based on my mom's frightening expression of interest, she hadn't expected to hear that. I almost missed her angry face. I definitely wasn't going anywhere tonight without answering questions now.

"I'm so sorry Alex! It just popped out." Sam put her hands up to her mouth.

I knew better than to buy her mock-shame act. She'd one hundred percent intended to let that nugget slip. Even in my distress, I could see it was a stroke of genius. No police officer wanted to get involved in stopping teenage girls obsessed with a party and a boy.

Even better, it was completely believable as a reason why we'd want to dash off without throwing any undue suspicion on us.

"Sure, you girls can leave. I'll contact you if we need any more information." He looked at me, biting back a smile and wiggled his eyebrows. "I hope you have a great night."

He actually *wiggled his eyebrows*.

My face felt like it was going to burst into flames and my voice was barely audible as I put the back of my hands against my cheeks in a vain attempt to cool them off. "Ermmm, thanks."

My mom moved from the table to stand beside me, resting her arm on my shoulders. "I'm sure you understand I'll need to leave as well. I have a lot to discuss with my daughter, from the sounds of it."

My mom and the officer shared a look, which seemed to promise she would perform a full interrogation of her own when I got home.

He smirked. "Absolutely, ma'am. If I could just get you to write down your names and numbers for me, I'll call if I need anything else. Once the woman wakes up, we'll follow up with her."

My mom nodded, forgetting to mention she knew who the woman was. I didn't blame her. We'd deal with the fall-out when Tracey woke up.

We quickly scribbled the requested information down as Sam retrieved her phone and said goodbye to the Andersons, who were holding hands under the table with matching be-mused expressions. I wasn't sure what kind of relationship they'd had prior to the events of last night, but recent events seemed to have brought them closer.

Fear of death can do that, I guess.

When I looked at Betty Crocker, I was surprised to see her motioning for me to follow her into the hall. Glancing at the others and finding they were still occupied with the officer, I drifted over, curiosity outweighing my distrust.

"What do you want?" I was cautious. I had no idea what to think about her now. She wasn't quite the evil witch I'd suspected, but neither did she seem completely good.

She gave me a pleasant smile. "I'm sure I don't have to impress upon you how important it is for you to be careful what you say to the nice officer. I may have sprinkled a little bit of...suggestion...into the beverages I gave them."

She dropped her sweetness and now her words were forceful and direct. I took a half-step back at the change, but relaxed when I realized she was trying to include me, not threaten me.

"Which means, you and your friend are the only ones other than myself who know what really happened tonight. I saw no need to dose you two. In general, no one ever believes teens." She shrugged, as if apologizing for her assessment.

I had to agree with her. No one ever listened to me, and I didn't need people thinking I was crazy. No way was I going to explain my turn as a zombie.

"So what do you want us to say? And why should we do what you want?" I crossed my arms, waiting for a good reason to lie.

"You're going to say exactly what I just told the nice officer. You and your friend came for a visit with your mom. The Andersons are my neighbors, who also popped by around the same time. We all had a nice glass of apple cider together and were just about to say goodbye when we heard a thump in the basement and found your mother's friend."

When I jumped, Betty gave me a satisfied look.

"Oh yes, I know all about her. Don't worry, she'll be fine. Just between the two of us, she may have had a soothing beverage shortly after arrival. Don't worry—it takes approximately a day to sleep off and she'll feel marvelous after. Cheapest spa vacation ever. Of course, it does mean she won't be enjoying any Halloween parties this year."

I thought about what she'd said. She was right about no one believing anything I said about zombies or how today had actually gone down. It was an easy trip from there to saying nothing at all, unless we wanted reputations for being crazy of course. It wasn't fair, but it was the way things were.

Besides, she looked so innocent, I'd believed her surprise was real when I'd told her about Tracey, and I hadn't trusted her to start with. No one would ever believe me over Mrs. Claus.

She gave me a look that was hard to read, but part of me wondered if it was regret. Why would she feel regret? It wasn't like there'd been any permanent complications. What would she be sorry for? Especially if she actually was evil, which I was still on the fence about.

"If you're ever interested in, well, I don't know, learning how to... cook." She stopped abruptly.

I turned to see we'd been joined by the officer. She blinked up at him with the same angelic smile before she looked at me again.

"Come back Wednesday night at five, sharp. We can start our lessons then."

This time when our eyes met, I didn't see any evil. Whether she'd intended me to or not, I saw a lonely old woman in front of me who was hoping I'd say yes to another visit. As I processed what was happening, a smile spread over my face.

"I... I think I'd like that."

This could be interesting.

My mom's voice wafted over from the front door. "Ready to go, Chickie?"

I nodded, waving at the old woman and walked over to Sam. "Is your costume ready for tonight?"

Sam gave me a rakish smile. "Oh, yeah. And it's totally amazing. Do you want to get ready at my house?"

I bit my lip and looked at my mom, who shook her head, then sighed and gave me a patient look.

"Fine. You can get ready at Sam's. But you both have to answer my questions first, *capice*?"

I nodded. "Absolutely. I'll tell you everything."

She had a right to know what happened. When I'd found out where she was, I'd been terrified. I could only imagine the kind of things a mom would worry about.

That didn't mean I was going to tell her everything though.

Sometimes, you had to fudge the details to protect the innocent.

With that thought in mind, I held a hand out to the officer. "Thanks, sir. Happy Halloween."

He shook my hand and waved as we left. "Enjoy the night, ladies!"

AS WE WALKED DOWN THE leaf-covered walk, I marveled at how much my life had changed in a single, strange day. My mom knew about my secret crush now, but that was the least of it. Once I teased out how much she remembered from the time before the beverage, I'd decide what else to tell her.

Would I attempt to explain how I'd woken up dead, craving the sweet flesh of vegetables? I wasn't so sure.

I had no idea what would happen next, but after today, I wasn't nearly as nervous about seeing Zach. Who knows? Maybe I'll ask *him* out.

With an extra bounce in my step, due to the boost of bravery being dead had given me, I walked into the quickly falling dusk with my mom and best friend.

I can't wait to see where tonight takes me.

Don't miss out!

Visit the website below and you can sign up to receive emails whenever H. M. Gooden publishes a new book. There's no charge and no obligation.

https://books2read.com/r/B-A-POWE-JLBBB

BOOKS 2 READ

Connecting independent readers to independent writers.

Did you love *I was a Teenage Vegetarian Zombie Detective*?
Then you should read *Zahara's Quest*[1] by H. M. Gooden!

[2]

The last thing Zahara expects to hear when she's summoned
home is that her family has been cursed.

As the truth behind the family legend becomes apparent,
things become even more bizarre.

Vowing to return a mysterious emerald necklace sent by an
aunt she's never met, she'll have to rely on the help of friends to
face the past and defeat an ancient foe.

---

1. https://books2read.com/u/3LpB90

2. https://books2read.com/u/3LpB90

It's a good thing she's got the stubbornness and cunning of a fox to see her through because if she doesn't succeed, her future will vanish forever.

Read more at https://www.hmgoodenauthor.com/.

About the Author

H. M. Gooden has always loved the world of books, but over the last few years a new story has begged to be told, and as a result, this series was born.

In between dealing with children and work, the majority of the actual writing happens between four and six am and involves multiple cups of coffee for inspiration.

You can always find me on Twitter, Facebook, Instagram, Bookbub and Goodreads.

I always love to hear from readers!

Read more at https://www.hmgoodenauthor.com/.